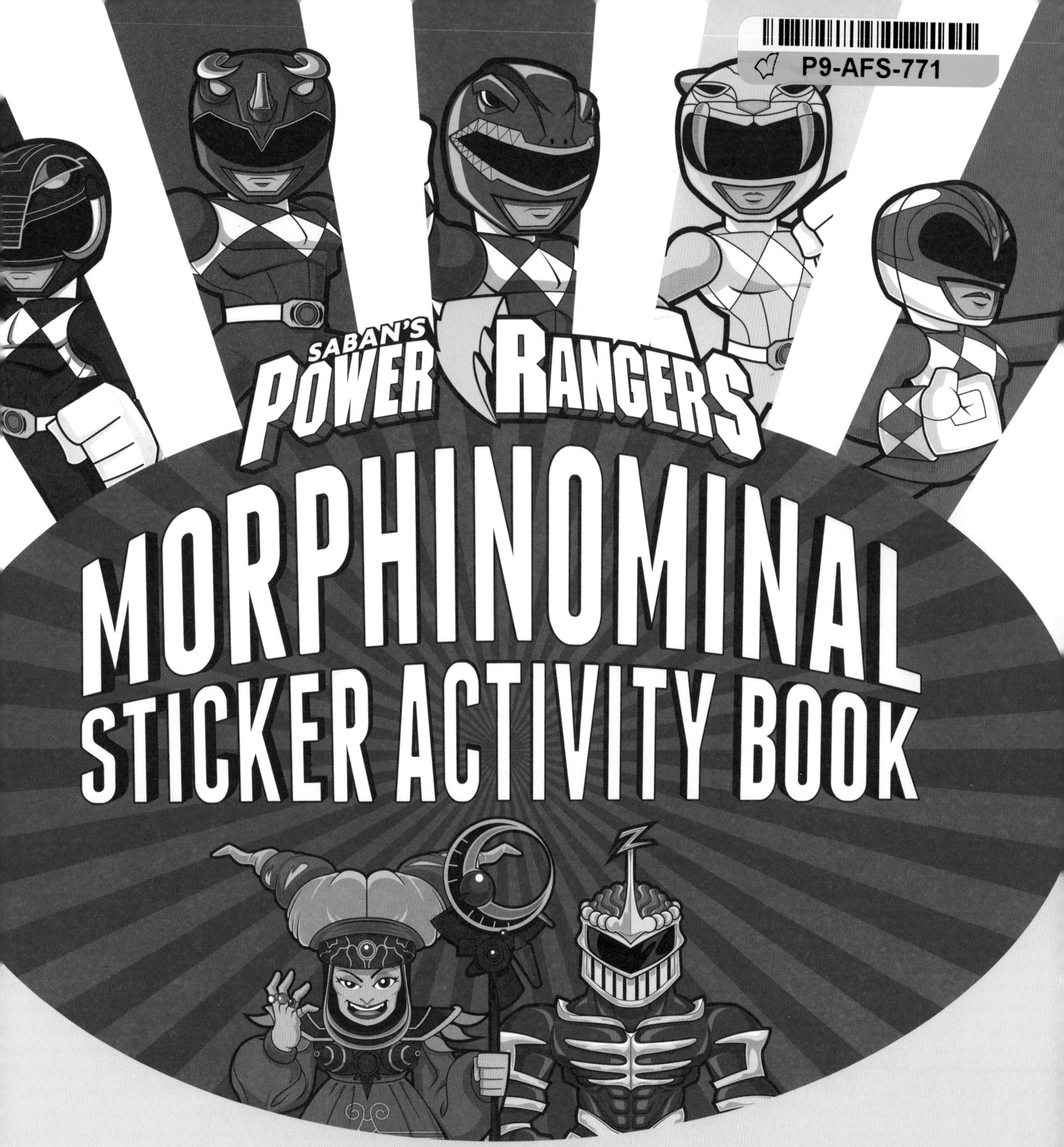

PENGUIN YOUNG READERS LICENSES
An Imprint of Penguin Random House LLC

Photo credits: pages 3, 13: (bubble) wellglad/iStock/Thinkstock; page 8: (maze) samarets1984/iStock/Thinkstock; page 9: (glass) nayneung1/iStock/Thinkstock; pages 10, 21: (cliffs) RomanKhomlyak/iStock/Thinkstock; pages 11, 20, 21: (moon) AvGusT174/iStock/Thinkstock; pages 19, 24: (Earth) leonello/iStock/Thinkstock; page 24: (maze) Mariyall/iStock/Thinkstock, (stars) maciek905/iStock/Thinkstock.

 Published by Penguin Young Readers Licenses, an imprint of Penguin Random House LLC, 345 Hudson Street, New York, New York 10014. Manufactured in China.

ISBN 9780515159899

10 9 8 7 6 5 4 3 2 1

GIVE ME SIX!

Meet the Mighty Morphin Power Rangers! Each Ranger has a unique Power Coin. Can you use stickers to match all of the Rangers with their Power Coins?

ALPHA 5

TREACHEROUS TEST

Rita Repulsa has the Green Ranger under her evil spell. Can you unscramble her nefarious, hypnotic messages?

RITA REPULSA

1. EB DOGO MRROOWTO

2. LLCHIIN HWIT HET ANVILIL

3. ABD SI DGOO EWNH REOUY A LIVLINA

4. RMOE NUF IGNEB DBA

5. EESHOR EEND AISNLLVI

MORPHINOMINAL!

Want to look like a Power Ranger?
Color the helmets on the next page, cut along the dotted lines (or ask a trusted Master to help), and tie strings on each side to wear it like a mask. Practice your skills below, and get to work, Ranger!

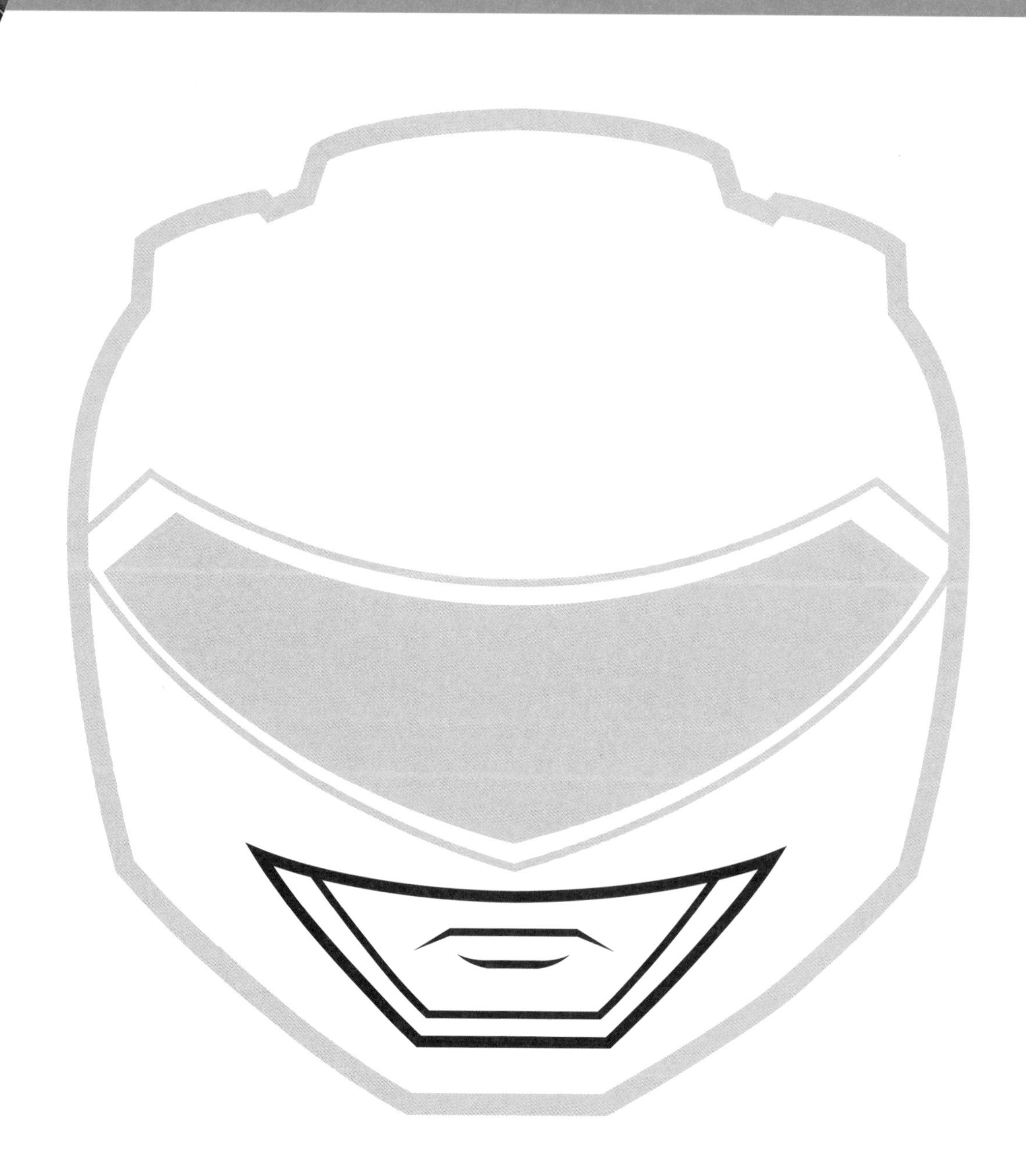

CREATE YOUR OWN HELMET!

CREATE YOUR OWN HELMET!

The Rangers are teaching Alpha 5 how to dance! They need some new music so they can really rock out.
Can you recommend some of your favorite songs?
DO THE ROBOT!
SONG TITLE
ARTIST
?

TRAINING TIME
The Rangers are all meeting at the Youth Center to train.
Using a different color for each Ranger, help them all find their way to the Youth Center!
Angel Grove
Youth Center
Gym
Juice Bar

THIRST QUENCHER

After a workout, the Rangers like to relax together over freshly squeezed juice. Design your own juice to sell at the Youth Center! Draw the fruits and veggies that you want to put in your juice and give it a catchy name!

INGREDIENTS

CATCHY JUICE NAME

FIGHTING BADDIES

Help! Lord Zedd and the Putty Patrollers are attacking Earth! Can you save the day? Use stickers of the Rangers and Zords to show their battle against the monsters.

MONSTER MASH

Lord Zedd is breeding new monsters to send down to Earth. Create a horrible monster here and draw it below.

MONSTER'S NAME:

MONSTER'S POWERS:

DINOZORD DUOS

When the biggest, scariest monsters attack, the Power Rangers are prepared! Each Ranger has the ability to control their own Dinozord. **Draw a line from each Ranger to their Zord. Then, place a lightning bolt sticker nearby to activate!**

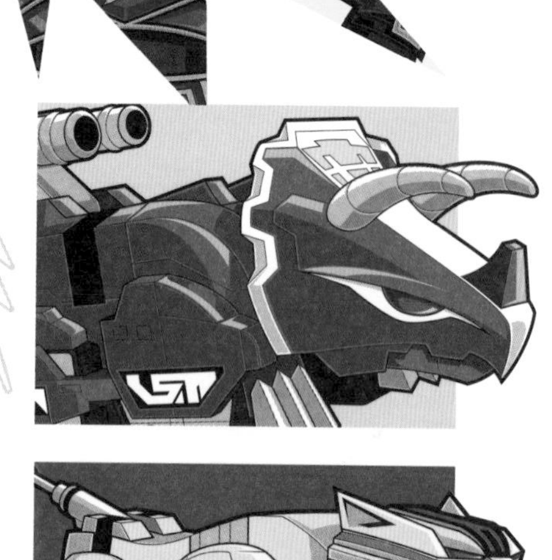

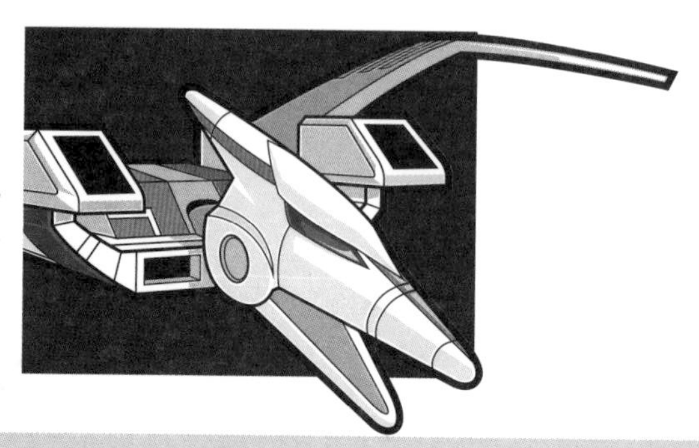

DAGGER DANGER

Rita Repulsa has stolen the Green Ranger's powerful Dragon Dagger! Zordon has sent the Rangers instructions to get it back, but some of the data is missing! Help them by filling in the blanks.

R__ta h__s giv__n

t__e D__ __ __ __o__

D__ __ge__ t__

G__ __d__r.

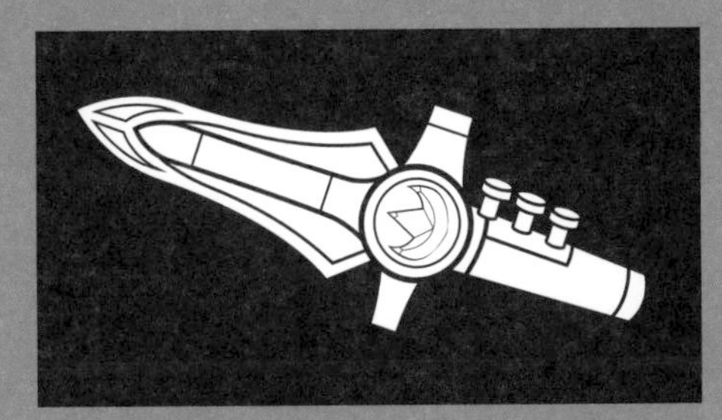

Hint:
Zordon's picture came through crystal clear. What is he saying about it?

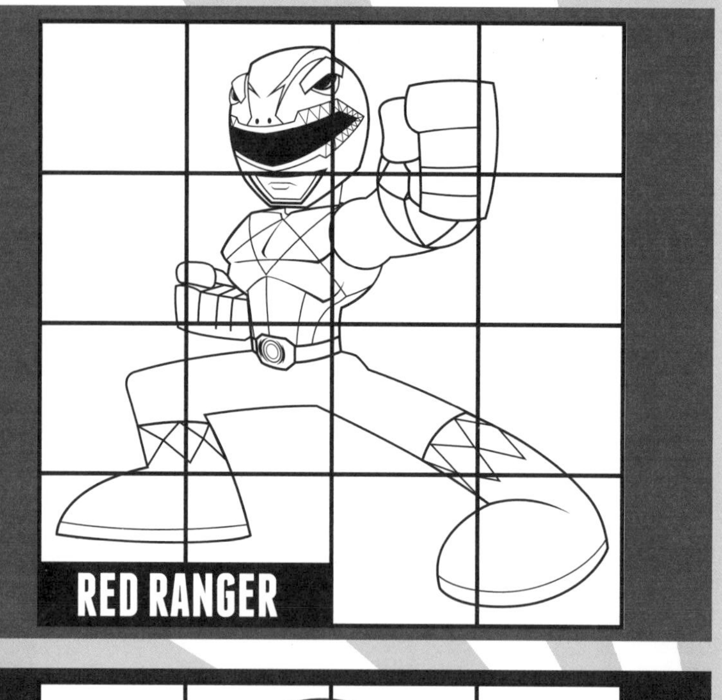
RED RANGER

PINK RANGER

BLACK RANGER

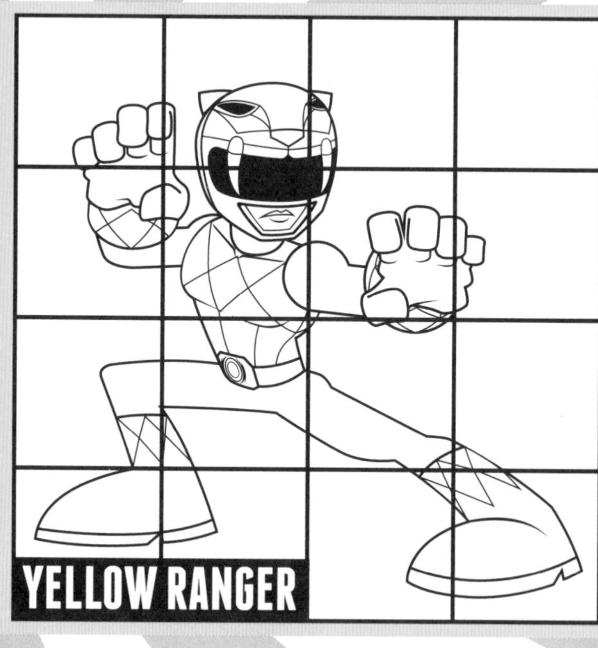
YELLOW RANGER

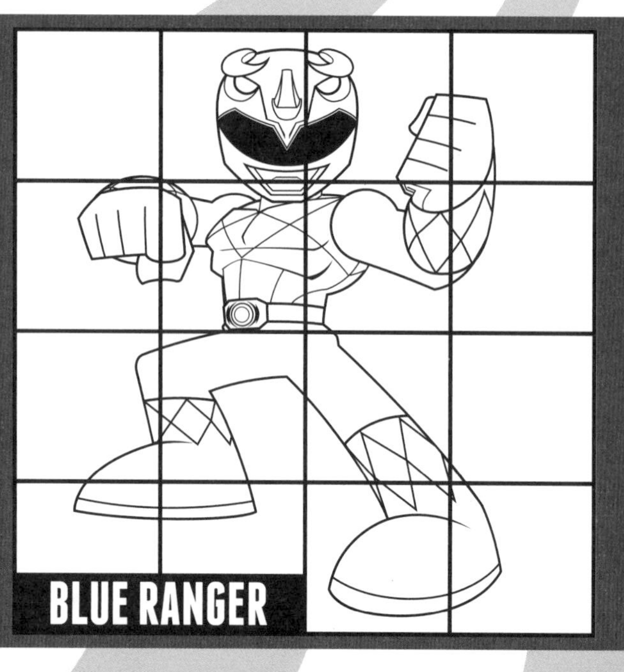
BLUE RANGER

GREEN RANGER

DRAWING LESSON

Learn to draw your favorite Power Rangers by using these grids!

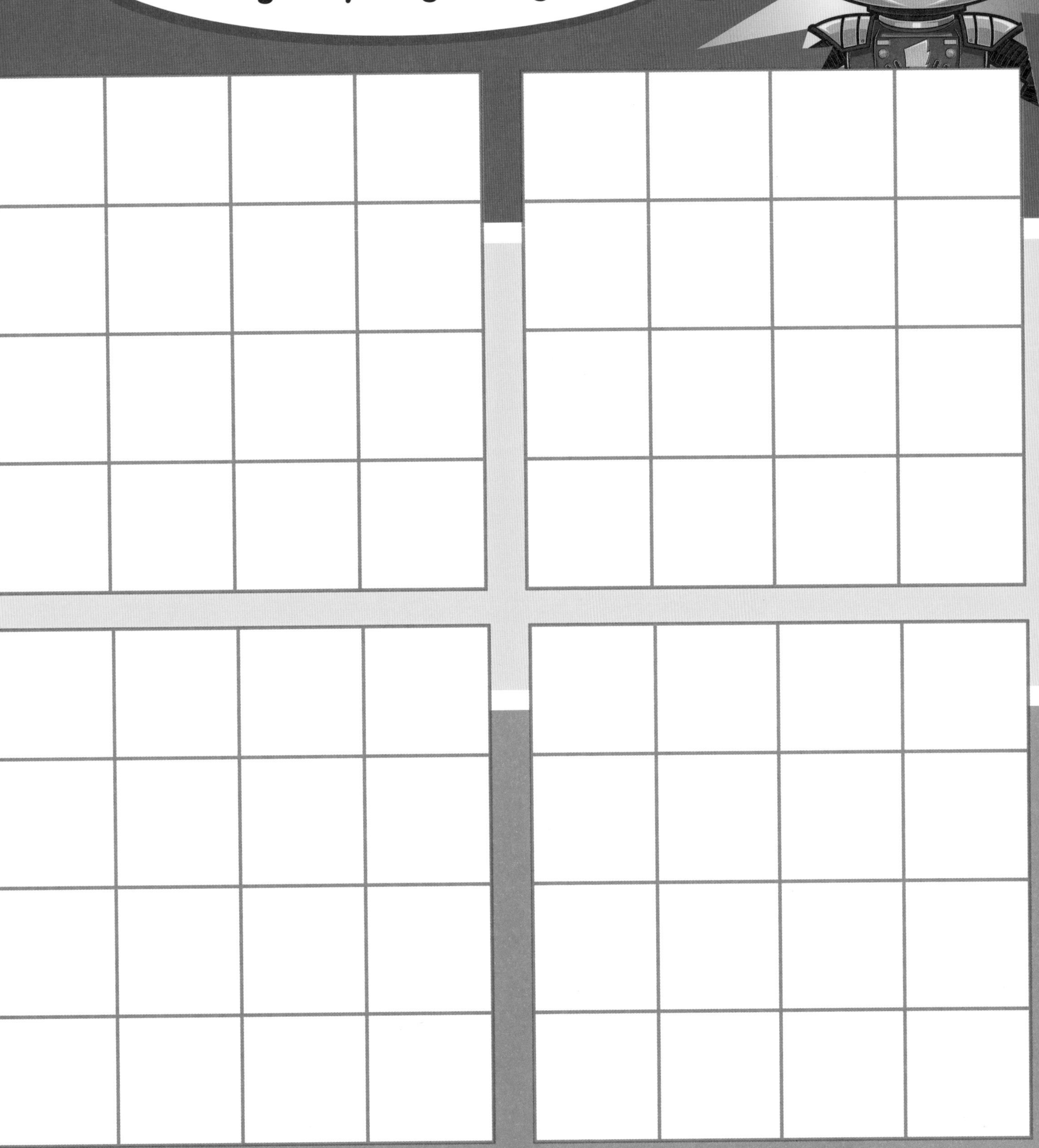

MEGAZORD MAKER

Someone has drained all the color from the Zords! Color in the super-powerful Megazord to restore its power.

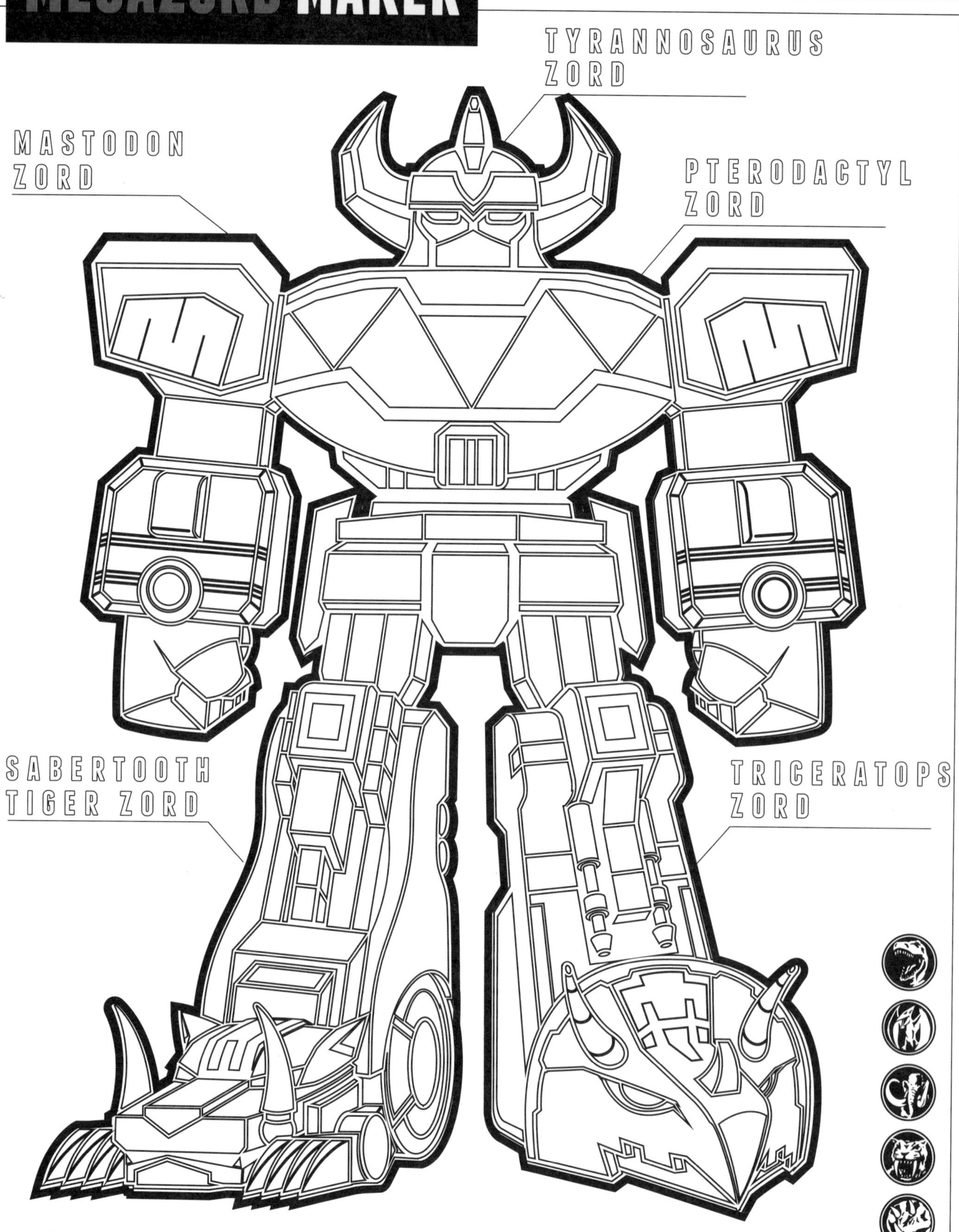

WHAT'S IN A NAME?

The Rangers may have superpowers, but they're still regular kids! Can you find their real names in this word search? When you do, place the Ranger's helmet sticker in their matching circle.

D	R	A	Z	Z	I	N	S	T	Q	Q	R	I	Y	D
K	X	J	C	R	A	N	O	I	Z	F	S	U	K	M
P	N	M	G	I	H	M	K	E	S	W	G	B	C	V
N	D	U	X	F	M	O	K	W	P	E	O	I	A	L
V	G	I	Q	Y	N	I	A	R	Y	Q	F	L	Z	K
M	B	I	B	D	M	C	I	E	C	T	G	L	Y	F
T	N	U	P	B	C	C	R	T	B	K	Z	Y	Y	P
A	Q	P	E	Y	D	Y	G	S	Q	U	A	T	T	E
R	G	R	Z	O	G	Y	B	N	O	S	A	J	Z	W
E	L	H	P	W	Q	D	B	I	G	E	F	O	A	J
Y	O	Y	O	F	J	L	U	F	A	T	O	J	T	H
P	E	O	R	J	A	K	S	P	J	A	R	Q	Q	F
Z	P	S	B	I	Q	S	G	I	I	X	B	I	V	F
O	S	Q	V	A	R	L	E	B	R	W	C	A	N	V
M	E	N	P	R	B	I	Q	O	C	H	L	G	V	I

POWER POSTERS

Make your own Power Rangers posters! Decorate the two scenes on the next sheet with words and stickers! When you're finished, cut out the page to hang it up in your bedroom. You can even flip it over depending on your mood!

SAVE THE WORLD!

HEROES NEED VILLAINS

SWITCHEROO

Trini has morphed into the Yellow Ranger!
Can you circle 11 differences between these two pictures?

QUIZMASTER

Which Ranger are you?

What are your favorite sports?

a) Weightlifting and any form of martial arts.
b) Dance
c) Gymnastics
d) I don't really like sports. I'd rather be reading.
e) Martial arts

Your friend is sad and you want to help them. What do you do?

a) Stay loyal and give advice.
b) Cheer them up by telling jokes.
c) Talk them through their problem and make sure they don't feel alone.
d) Ask them why they are sad, and then search for a solution to their problem.
e) Listen.

What do you do for fun?

a) Play sports.
b) Go to parties and spend time with friends.
c) Theater, dance, and music.
d) Play video games and explore the Internet.
e) Spend time outside! I love going to the beach or taking walks through the woods.

What would be the greatest birthday present ever?

a) A training session with your favorite athlete.
b) Tickets to a sold-out concert.
c) A guitar.
d) A new video-game system.
e) A tropical vacation with your best friend.

IF YOU PICKED:

MOSTLY A'S:

You are the Red Ranger!
You are loyal, giving, and a star athlete.

MOSTLY B'S:

You are the Black Ranger!
You are funny, kind, and friends with everybody you meet.

MOSTLY C'S:

You are the Pink Ranger!
You are talented, caring, and outgoing.

MOSTLY D'S:

You are the Blue Ranger!
You are inventive, intelligent, and sweet.

MOSTLY E'S:

You are the Yellow Ranger!
You are smart, loving, and brave.

DOWN TO EARTH

Lord Zedd is chasing the Rangers across the galaxy! Help them escape and safely return to Earth.

I DON'T

GSV DVWWRMT

___ _______

LU IRGZ IVKFOHZ

__ ____ _______

ZMW OLIW AVWW

___ ____ ____

DROO YV SVOW

____ __ ____

ZG GSV EROOZRM

__ ___ _______

HLXRZO XOFY

______ ____

Z + R

A=Z	N=M
B=Y	O=L
C=X	P=K
D=W	Q=J
E=V	R=I
F=U	S=H
G=T	T=G
H=S	U=F
I=R	V=E
J=Q	W=D
K=P	X=C
L=O	Y=B
M=N	Z=A

GET ACTIVE!

The Rangers all love to exercise, but they each have a different sport of choice. How do you like to stay fit? Match the Rangers to their favorite forms of exercise.

GYMNASTICS

YOGA

MARTIAL ARTS

LIFTING BOOKS

DANCE

WEIGHT TRAINING

PINK RANGER

The Power Rangers work together and help one another whenever possible.

Have you ever helped a friend in need? Write your story here.

TEAMWORK RULES

Power Rangers must stay sharp all the time. How alert are you?
Test your memory by staring at this picture for at least a minute.

Cover it up and answer these questions:

1. Which Zord is missing from the picture?
2. What color is the Tyrannosaurus Zord?
3. How many lightning bolts are in the picture?
4. Which way is the Sabertooth Tiger Zord facing?

CREATE A CARD!

Do you have a friend who loves the Power Rangers as much as you do? Make their day by sending them a card! Color and decorate the card below, and then cut it out of the page, stick it in an envelope, and send it on its way!

UNTIL NEXT TIME!
SABAN'S POWER RANGERS
The Power Rangers thank you for all your help! Color in the Rangers and wish them luck on their next mission!

3

1. BE GOOD TOMORROW
2. CHILLIN WITH THE VILLAIN
3. BAD IS GOOD WHEN YOU'RE A VILLAIN
4. MORE FUN BEING BAD
5. HEROES NEED VILLAINS

8

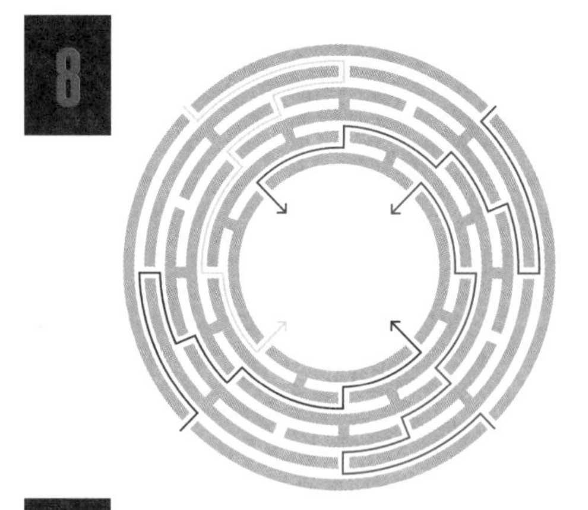

12

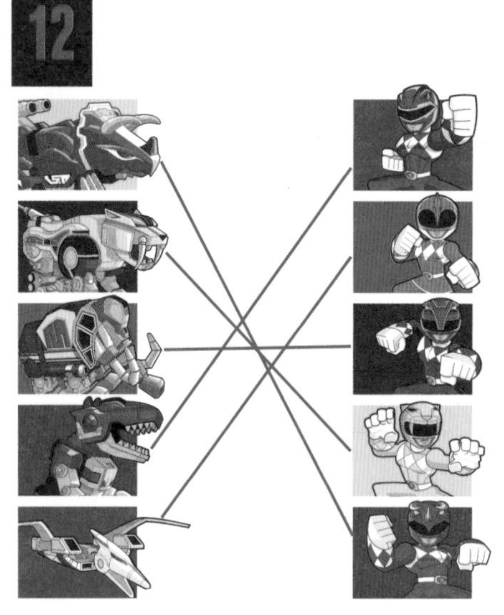

13

Rita has given the Dragon Dagger to Goldar.

17

21

24

25

The wedding of Rita Repulsa and Lord Zedd will be held at the Villain Social Club.

26